Nikki McClure

MAMA, IS IT SUMMER YET?

Abrams Books for Young Readers, New York

Mama, is it summer yet?

Not yet, my little one.
But the buds are swelling.
Soon new leaves will unfold.

Mama, is it summer yet?

Not yet, my little one.
But the squirrel is building her nest.
Soon her babies will be born.

Mama, is it summer yet?

Not yet, my little one.
But the earth is soft.
Soon the seeds will sprout and root.

Mama, is it summer yet?

Not yet, my little one.
But the swallows are singing.
Soon warmer winds will blow.

Mama, is it summer yet?

Not yet, my little one.
But the ducklings are following their mother.
Soon they will grow big and bold.

Mama, is it summer yet?

Not yet, my little one.
But the trees are blossoming.
Soon tiny apples will appear.

Mama, is it summer now?

Yes! Oh yes, my little one!
The honeybees are in the flowers.
The sun is warm on your round belly.
The berries are juicy and sweet.

My little one, it is summer now!

For my mother.

—N.M.

Thank you to Susan Van Metre and Georgia Munger
for their help with finding the right words and pictures.

Artist's Note

The illustrations are cut paper. First, I draw the image on black paper, and then I cut it out with an X-Acto knife. I try to keep everything connected by a path of black paper. The paper becomes lace-like as the image emerges. I decide the width of line and what will be black or white as I cut. There is no erasing, so if I make a mistake, I just have to keep cutting and find a solution. The cut paper is then scanned, and color is added by digitally.

Library of Congress Cataloging-in-Publication Data

McClure, Nikki.
Mama, is it summer yet? / by Nikki McClure.
p. cm.
Summary: As spring slowly turns to summer, a little boy builds a fort and plants
a garden in impatient anticipation.
ISBN 978-0-8109-8468-4
[1. Summer—Fiction. 2. Seasons—Fiction.] I. Title.
PZ7.M4784141946Mam 2010
[E]—dc22
2009023013

Text and illustrations copyright © 2010 Nikki McClure
Book design by Chad W. Beckerman

Printed and bound in U.S.A.
10 9 8 7 6 5 4 3 2 1

THE ART OF BOOKS SINCE 1949

115 West 18th Street
New York, NY 10011
www.abramsbooks.com